I AM A SITH

For Nick, my Darth Dad
—C.N.

By Christopher Nicholas
Illustrated by Chris Kennett

 A GOLDEN BOOK • NEW YORK

randomhousekids.com
ISBN 978-0-7364-3607-6 (trade) — ISBN 978-0-7364-3608-3 (ebook)

Printed in the United States of America

10 9 8 7 6 5 4 3 2 1

I am a Sith.

I am a master of evil.

Sith are **dark warriors** who crave power. They spread fear and try to enslave all those around them.

A Sith's evil power comes from the dark side of the **Force**—an energy field that has been twisted by anger and hate.

Sith can use the dark side to attack their enemies . . .

. . . and create lightning from their fingertips!

Every Sith has a **lightsaber**—a powerful laser sword that can cut through anything!

Slash!

The energy blade
of a Sith lightsaber is
always **red**.

The Sith are masters of trickery and lies.
Darth Sidious concocted a war to create his
own **clone army**.

He took control of the Galactic Republic—
and declared himself the **Emperor**!

Sith are the sworn enemies of the **Jedi Knights**, guardians of peace.

After the Clone Wars, the Sith sent out
special agents—called **Inquisitors**—to
find and eliminate every Jedi in the galaxy!

Throughout the ages, there have been many **dark-side warriors**. But not all of them have been true Sith.

There can only be two Sith at one time—
a **master** and an **apprentice**. One to
embody power, and the other to crave it.

Darth Maul was the first apprentice to Darth Sidious.

Piloting his **Sith Interceptor**, Darth Maul traveled throughout the galaxy to do his master's evil bidding.

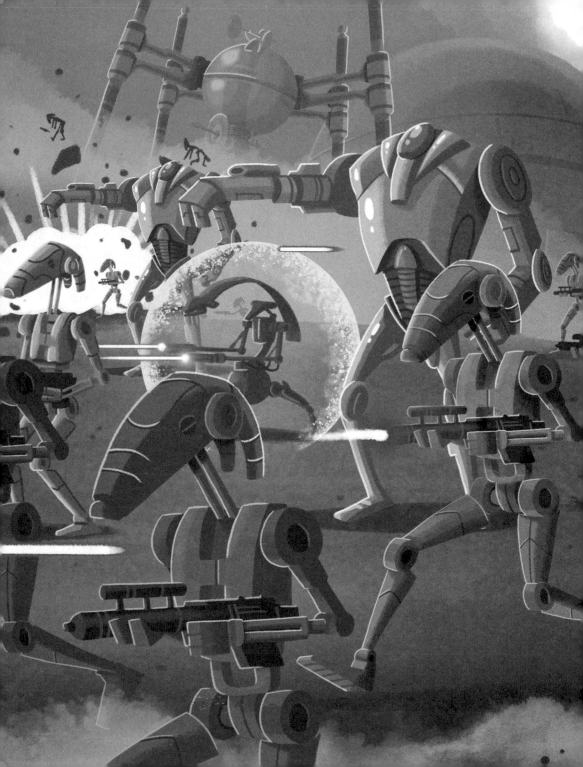

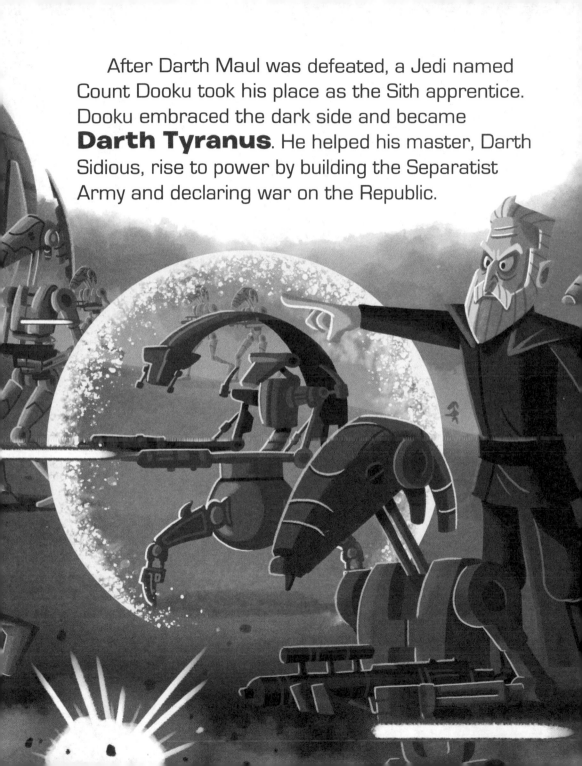

After Darth Maul was defeated, a Jedi named Count Dooku took his place as the Sith apprentice. Dooku embraced the dark side and became **Darth Tyranus**. He helped his master, Darth Sidious, rise to power by building the Separatist Army and declaring war on the Republic.

But Darth Sidious's most powerful Sith apprentice, by light-years, was . . . **Darth Vader**! With Vader by his side, Darth Sidious formed the Galactic Empire and took control of the galaxy.

Darth Vader was once a Jedi Knight named **Anakin Skywalker**. Darth Sidious preyed upon Anakin's fears with lies and tricked him into joining the dark side. Anakin betrayed his master, **Obi-Wan Kenobi**—and the entire Jedi Order!

Darth Vader escaped the evil clutches of the dark side. He was **redeemed** when he saved his son, Luke Skywalker, from Darth Sidious.

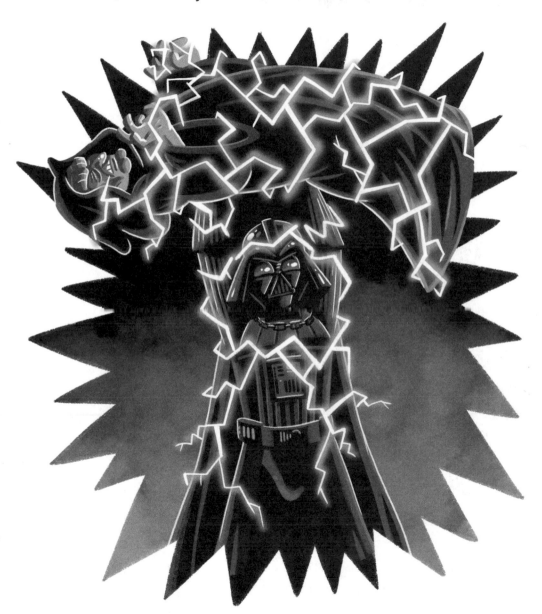

Vader destroyed the Emperor and brought peace to the galaxy. The dark side of the Force was gone forever. **Or was it . . . ?**